The Worst House

Written by Susan Griffiths

Illustrated by Betty Greenhatch

Rigby

The Worst House

With these characters ...

Mrs. Juniper

Mrs. Dimple

Slurpy

Sniff

"It was a massive

Every year, the "Cleanest Street Competition" is held. Every year, the neighbors on Barlow Street hope that their street will win.

But Barlow Street is spoiled by the junk in the front yard of number 41. It seems Barlow Street will never win . . . until Mrs. Juniper and Mrs. Dimple have an idea!

mountain of junk!"

Chapter 1.

"It's almost time for the competition!" said Mrs. Juniper loudly. "Look at all that junk," she said quietly.

"Only a week to go!" said Mrs. Dimple heartily. "That house is the worst eyesore," she whispered.

Mrs. Dimple
rubbed her forehead
and said,
"Tut-tut-tut."

Every evening, as the sun went down, Mrs. Juniper and Mrs. Dimple walked their dogs, Slurpy and Sniff.

They crossed the road from the empty
house at 41 Barlow Street. They
whispered another, "Tut-tut-tut."

The other houses in Barlow Street
looked like dolls' houses. They had tidy
front yards and colorful flower beds.

On their way home, they stopped at
number 41 for a closer look. No one
had lived in the house for many years.
The windows were too dirty to see
through. The lawn was overgrown and
littered with junk.

There were old TV antennas. There was a rusty white bathtub. There were old black car tires.

There were sheets of red iron. There were striped pink mattresses with fluffy white stuffing bursting out of them. There were crumpled cardboard boxes, planks of wood, and soft-drink cans. It was a massive mountain of junk!

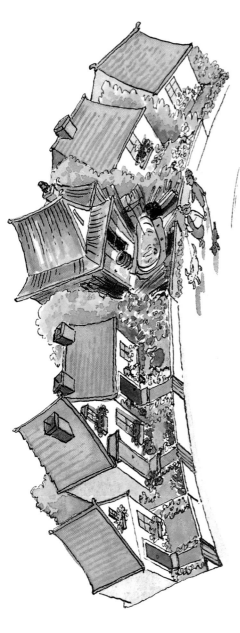

"Barlow Street will never win the Cleanest Street Competition," said Mrs. Juniper sadly.

"How can we win when our street is always spoiled by number 41? It is like a rotten tooth in a row of white teeth," said Mrs. Dimple, feeling upset.

The two neighbors tut-tut-tutted, as their dogs pulled them along.

Every year, each neighbor tried to make Barlow Street the cleanest street in town. They tidied their front yards and planted flowers.

Every year, the judges walked along the street, checking their judging forms until they came to number 41. They always stopped checking and would tut-tut-tut, too.

Chapter 2.

The next evening, Mrs. Juniper, Mrs. Dimple, Slurpy, and Sniff met outside number 41. The sunset was turning orange.

"Look at all that junk," said Mrs. Juniper softly. "What can we do?"

"Yes, it's *still* an eyesore," whispered Mrs. Dimple.

Both neighbors shook their heads
and said, "Tut-tut-tut."

"I could put my topiary swan
in the front yard before the judging
on Saturday," said Mrs. Juniper.
She thought that the judges might look
at the swan and not the junk.

But that would only work if the
judging took place at night, and
the judges were wearing sunglasses!

While the two neighbors talked, Slurpy and Sniff ran into the messy front yard. Slurpy pulled out some of the white stuffing from a mattress. Sniff poked his nose into a cardboard box full of tin cans.

The dogs enjoyed being off their leashes. They enjoyed making even more of a mess at 41 Barlow Street, until . . .

"Bad dogs!" growled Mrs. Juniper. Slurpy had white fluffy stuffing in his mouth. "And look at what your dog has stuck on his nose!"

"Slurpy looks like the mayor, and Sniff looks like the mayor's old car," said Mrs. Dimple, pointing at them.

Suddenly, before they could say
a tut-tut-tut, Mrs. Dimple had an idea.
She looked at Slurpy and Sniff, and
the mountain of junk. She began
to whisper to Mrs. Juniper.

And this time, the two neighbors
were not tut-tut-tutting, but
whispering and looking very excited.

Chapter 3.

The next morning, the other neighbors peered out their windows. They heard clattering and banging sounds coming from number 41.

They saw Mrs. Juniper digging up the junk with a spade. Mrs. Dimple could be seen poking around the junk with a pitchfork.

"Here's something red!" said
Mrs. Juniper in a high, excited voice.

"Here's something white!" said
Mrs. Dimple in a soft, happy voice.

They heaved and hauled the junk
into neat piles.

One by one, the other neighbors came over to help them. The massive mountain of junk slowly became lots of miniature mounds of junk.

"Hey, Mrs. Juniper! This bath looks like the one you had in your house," called out her neighbor, Ted.

Mrs. Juniper's face turned red. "It couldn't be," she replied, a little too quickly.

"Hey, Ben! These tires look like the ones you had on your car," said Mrs. Dimple to another neighbor.

Ben's face turned red. He pretended to look shocked. "No, surely not," he replied, a little too quietly.

"Excuse me, Mrs. Dimple. This red iron reminds me of your garden shed," said Dina, another neighbor.

Mrs. Dimple's face turned red, too. "That's not possible," she replied, walking away a little too quickly.

From then on, no one said they recognized *any* of the junk.

By that evening, everyone was exhausted. But not too exhausted to look up proudly at their work.

Before today, they hoped the judges would wear sunglasses and judge the competition at night. Now, they hoped the sun would shine brightly on Saturday.

Chapter 4.

It was the big day, at last! The judges walked up Barlow Street and carefully checked their judging forms.

When they came to 41 Barlow Street, the judges stopped. They couldn't take their eyes off the amazing sight before them. The neighbors fell silent. Would number 41 get its first check ever?

There it was — a towering sculpture of the mayor, as tall as the house. His pants were made of old black tires. His jacket was made of sheets of iron. His face was made of striped pink mattress material. And his beard was made of fluffy white mattress stuffing.

Beside him was an old car made out of a rusty white bathtub and planks of wood. In front on the hood stood an ornament made from a can and some flowers. The grill was made of old TV antennas.

The judges smiled as they whispered to each other. Everyone from Barlow Street knew that this was a good sign.

Just then, the huge mayor creaked. Would it stand up for a little longer?

One of the judges turned to the neighbors.

"Congratulations to all of you," said the judge. "We have never seen anything like . . . *that*!" she said, pointing at number 41.

"We all agree that the "Cleanest Street Competition" has been won by . . . Barlow Street!"

That afternoon, Mrs. Juniper, Mrs. Dimple, and all their neighbors held a big street party. Everyone celebrated winning first prize.

They celebrated for hours outside
the empty house at number 41:
the cleanest house on the street!

"The Judges Decide"

Like a rotten tooth,
In a row of white,
The house at 41
Is a dreadful sight.

But the messy front yard
Is full of surprises,
And from all the junk
A statue rises.

The neighbours work hard,
All through the day.
They all wonder what
The judges will say.

The forms are checked,
And everyone grins,
When the judges decide
That Barlow Street wins!